DRIEHOEK

A young adult paranormal thriller

BRADLEY CHARBONNEAU

Credits

Cover Photo by Oliver Ragfelt on Unsplash

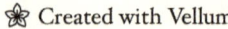 Created with Vellum

I'm just the messenger here—and you know what they say about the messenger?

Don't shoot me.

FOREWORD

This is a *really* short book.

If you were expecting a really long book, this isn't that book. In fact, it's so short, you might be done before you stand up again.

> "Bradley, why did you write such a short
> book?"

Crazy, I know.

But I'm trying to write like I enjoy reading: in smaller pieces. A 847-page tome is daunting to me. I want something I can manage, I can take in, that has a short story feel with the promise of more to come.

Li & Lu have been MIA. They've been busy. But while in Austria last fall as I was working on Charlie Holiday's new series, Li & Lu forced their way into my mind as if they were the jealous brothers who weren't getting the attention. Which was true.

"The true sign of intelligence is not knowledge but imagination."

— ALBERT EINSTEIN

"A terrific adventure with a very unusual premise. A gem."

PRAISE FOR BRADLEY CHARBONNEAU

(PREVIOUS BOOKS)

"Deliciousness for the soul."

> — PEGGY C. (ON EVERY SINGLE DAY)

"This fine book encourages us to take a very deep breath, start afresh, and make or lives what they CAN be."

> — GRADY HARP, AMAZON "HALL OF FAME" TOP 100 REVIEWER (ON EVERY SINGLE DAY)

"The suspense carries the tale along and in the end leaves the reader to ponder about unresolved mysteries."

> — A. KUGUSHEV (ON THE SECRET OF KITE HILL)

"Good mystery."

> — R. A. MCKAY (ON THE SECRET OF KITE HILL)

REQUEST

I know. We haven't even started. I'll be quick.

Book reviews.

They make or break the success of a book—and an author.

I'll just give it to you straight: **I love writing**. I want to write full time. I am determined to be an author. If you don't believe me, you haven't read "Every Single Day." I don't give up easily—if ever.

But I can't do it alone.

EVERY SINGLE BOOK REVIEW IS PRECIOUS TO PROSPECTIVE READERS.

If at any moment as you read this book you have a fleeting glimpse of something positive (a laugh, an insight, a moment of enjoyment as Lu twists the plot, *anything*), please write it up on the site where you bought this book.

That's it. That's my request.

Thank you.

PROLOGUE

Li & Lu are back.

It's been a while. They've been busy. Moving to Holland, enrolling in new schools, new basketball teams.

Apparently Lu has been working on his paranormal abilities (who knew!? ... that's a paranormal joke) while Li has been studying ... math.

I know. I know.

Both seem preposterous. But which one sounds more feasible? Both defy conventional wisdom and I personally have no idea. Remember:

I'm just the messenger.

I wish I could say that I came up with the story lines and weaved them into the perilous suspense thrillers that they have become. But alas, I just "download" the information and it comes through my fingers and onto the page.

A few words from Lu.

A comment from Li.

And we're off to the races.

You see, they are boys. They don't communicate. Well, not in the way girls do. Most boys use two syllables and call that dialogue. Others, like Lu, can't be quieted even with an acoustic foam cube.

I digress.

Li & Lu are back.

They're ready for action.

And yet again, the dog. The poor dog. He means well. But he just manages to get into trouble. Then again, he's a dog.

And they are boys. It's a mathematical certainty that there will be adventure.

Li & Lu are going to work together like never before. They're almost friends. They almost like each other.

Almost.

Welcome to book number five of Li & Lu: Driehoek.

For Luca

DRIEHOEK

1

WHEN DOES THE NEXT ADVENTURE START?

AND WHO'S INVOLVED?

"We cannot solve our problems with the same thinking we used when we created them."

— ALBERT EINSTEIN

"Lu Holiday, it's great to have you on the show," the interviewer said a sthey sat down on the metal bench on the edge of the school playground. "I'm Meghan Cumberbun from the Shining Stars Podcast."

"It's great to be here," Lu said, but then looked around. "Well, here, I don't know about here here like the playground of my school, but it's really great to be on your show," he stopped then started again. "I also just really wanted to say 'It's great to be here.'"

"Have you heard of the show?"

"Uh, no, I don't really know what a podcast is."

"It's like a radio show, but then you can listen whenever you want."

"I don't really know what a radio show is either."

"Oh."

"Twee voeten op een zijkant van je fiets, Kim," Lu shouted out towards the middle of the playground where it looked like school was just getting out.

"Sorry," Meghan said, "What did you say?"

"I told that girl right there, Kim, in the jeans, that she was not supposed to sit on her bike on the playground, she needs to walk it and have two feet on one side of the bike."

"So you speak Dutch?"

"Well, uh, yeah," Lu looked at her with his mouth agape and continued and he opened his palm upwards and scanned the area as if showing the interviewer where they were. "This is Holland."

"Oh, I thought maybe you were in an international school or something, since you moved here."

"Nope, eek pra-aat de Nay-der-lunds oak," Lu said and had a huge smile on his face as if what he said was not only genius but tremendously hilarious at the same time. Which, of course, it was.

"Sorry, Lu, what did you say?"

"It was a joke."

"Was it funny?"

"The funniest," Lu said and almost couldn't get a sentence out straight. "I said that I spoke Dutch but I said it in Dutch but with a terrible American accent. It was really funny. You should have been there."

"But I was here."

"Oh yeah."

Meghan looked to the cameraman with a face that said

something like 'I think this is going to be the shortest or the longest interview of my career.' The cameraman motioned with his hand to keep it going.

"Can I ask a question, Mrs. Cumberbatch?"

"Miss Cumberbun, but yes, go right ahead, Lu."

"If this is a podcast, that's just, like, listening, right? So why is there a cameraman?"

"Wow, great question, Lu!" Meghan shifted on the hard metal bench happy to get off of topics with languages she didn't understand and answer a question she knew.

"We also publish the interviews on YouTube so we can reach that audience, too."

"Oh, so I'll be on YouTube?"

"You sure will," Meghan said with a Disney-esque over-the-top happy smile and enthusiasm.

"How's my hair?" Lu asked and pulled his hand through his longish blond hair and looked towards the camera as if it was a mirror and turned his head this way and that for the best angle.

"You look mah-ve-lous," Meghan said but the reference was lost on 11-year-old Lu.

"Oh, good," Lu said and then looked right at Meghan. "So, when do we start the interview?"

Meghan leaned in towards Lu a bit and whispered, "We already have."

"Oh."

"So, Lu, I heard through the grapevine that you might be starring in a new series of stories."

"Seriously? Wow," he nodded as he processed the news. "But what's the grapevine and how do you hear through it? Isn't that where grapes grow?"

"Excellent point, Lu. Yes, it's a vine where grapes grow but, wow, how do you explain that? It's when you hear something from someone else about something else and maybe it's like it travels through the vine of grapes from one person to the other and gets to you and then you heard it through the grapevine," and Meghan seemed to go out of interview mode for a moment, looked up and to her right and thought she might not have said this part aloud, but she did. "I never really thought about it. Wow, that's kinda cool."

"Oh. That is cool."

"So is it true?"

"Is what true?"

"That you're going to be in a new series of stories?"

"I don't know, is it true?"

"Didn't your dad tell you?"

"He's in Austria."

"In Austria?"

"Austria. He's at some castle."

"Oh, that sounds fun," she thought back to her research. "Wow, you guys sure have a thing with castles."

"Well, he's at a workshop."

"In a castle?"

"Yeah."

"Cool."

"At least that's what he tells us kids. Who knows what he's really doing. As far as you know, he's just a regular, mild-mannered accountant."

"Do you know what mild-mannered means, Lu?"

"No, I got it from Superman."

"Oh dear," she said with a sigh that covered her entire

romantic life and even went through the phase with that Billy Donovan and why they never had kids. She regained her composure and remembered she was still sitting with a kid. Even though the kid said stuff like mild-mannered. "But are you still really a kid, Lu?" she asked and put a hand on her hip and did her best job of being friends with a kid.

"I'm 11."

"Is that a kid?"

"I hope so," he said. "I like being a kid."

"What do you like about being a kid?"

"I get to play basketball, see into the minds of people, play video games, and I don't have to have a job."

"Sorry, what was that second one?"

"Video games? Yeah, I like this football one where they beat each other up on the field and there are excellent sound effects of grunts and–"

"No, the seeing into minds of people."

"Oh yeah, that one," Lu said and looked out onto the playground. "Niels, niet op je fiets! Naast je fiets. Zo meteen is er straf, hoor."

Meghan let all of that Dutch slide on by and continued her interrogation. "Right. Yes, so you play basketball and video games and see into the minds of people?"

"Yeah," Lu kept his eyes on the playground. He had a job to do and he wasn't about to let some interview get him fired. "I have a fantastic 3-point shot. It's tremendous. I'm the best shooter on the team."

"Did you just say tremendous? Where'd you get that word?"

"You don't want to know," Lu said and kept a stern eye on the playground.

"But about the seeing into the minds of people?"

"Yeah, I can do that, too. But not all the time."

"Oh."

"Yeah, that's kinda cool."

"But what do you mean exactly? What happens? Can you tell us a little about it?"

"Well, I don't really know how it all works to be honest with you."

"Because you weren't being honest earlier but now you are?"

"Huh?" Lu looked at her, confused. "No, I was honest then and I'm honest now."

"Just checking," Meghan said and winked to the camera. The cameraman smiled and rolled his eyes.

"But what can you see when you look into people's minds?"

"Well, I can't always do it. I don't really know when I can't and when I can. But sometimes I can and sometimes I can't," Lu was about to bark orders to a kid on the playground but the kid saw Lu's evil eye and hopped off his bike. Lu gave him the thumbs up.

"Can you see into my mind right now, Lu Holiday?"

"Well, yeah, I guess so, but it's kinda foggy. I'm a little distracted at the moment."

"Because you're a little nervous about being in an interview that's going to go to millions of people on YouTube and the podcast?"

"No, because, do you see that girl over there? Her name is Salem. She's always trying to sneak by me when

I'm on playground duty and she just got on the playground so I'm keeping an eagle eye on her," Lu paused. "She's always up to something." He just kept going. "When she's on playground duty I do the same, so I guess it's kind of a thing we do."

"Don't let me interrupt," Meghan said and gave her cameraman a 'Can you believe this kid?' look but the cameraman motioned by rolling his hand over and over that she should keep going.

"Miss Cumberbond?"

"Cumberbun."

"Do you have a blue car?"

"Uh, yes," she was physically taken aback.

"There's a narrow country road with trees on both sides and a blue car," Lu said as he turned his gaze from the lawless playground and stared into the eyes of the woman sitting next to him. "Just be careful driving home tonight."

"Why? What? What are you talking about?"

"Salem, I see you!" Lu's attention was back on the playground. "I see you sitting on your saddle. I'm afraid I'm going to have to deduct points for that infraction." There was screaming in English from a young girl that took over the decibels in the vicinity. Then it stopped abruptly.

"No more Dutch?"

"She speaks some English," Lu said, his laser focus unwavering on Salem's next move. Meghan nodded.

"Just keep moving, Salem. You're on duty tomorrow, right? We'll see if you can catch me," Lu said and was clearly enjoying the interaction.

"Could we get back to the car and the trees and being

careful tonight, Lu?" Meghan asked leaning in closer to the boy as he raised his hand and pointed a finger at another student on the school yard.

"Well, that's all I saw, so, yeah, well, that's all I know," Lu turned back to his interview. "But can I ask another question?"

"Sure," she said, still a little rattled.

"Through that grapevine, what did you say you heard?"

"That there's another adventure for you in the works, that you're going to be in a new story."

"Oh man, that's so cool!" Lu turned back to her.

"So you're excited?"

"Oh man, yes, so much," he didn't look at her and didn't seem to be looking at the playground, but was just staring into the space ahead of him.

"I really miss being in adventures. Did you hear about that time we were in that caste in Ireland?"

"I did, Lu."

"That was so scary! But also super cool. I mean, the whole thing in the dungeon and Alistair and the secrets from the past, but like hundreds of years ago. Man, those were the days."

"Yeah, woo," Meghan said, still slightly distracted by the whole blue car and tree-lined street thing Lu seemed to just gloss over. "Where do you think the next story will take place? Or what's going to happen?"

"How am I supposed to know?"

"Well, weren't you part of the others?"

"Oh yeah, you're right. I guess so."

"What would you like the next adventures to be about? Where would you like to go or what would you like to do?"

"What if we went to the moon and then there were dragons and machine guns and--"

"But I thought the adventures were real?"

"Oh, they are."

"So the moon and dragons?"

"Well, that's what I would like."

"You like the moon and dragons."

"Well, dragons I just said because I was being silly but I'm not really a big dragon fan."

"So, Lu Holiday--"

"Why do you sometimes say my last name?"

Meghan was taken aback yet again by this young boy who was only half paying attention to her and half looking for law-breaking pre-teens on the playground who he could write up.

"I don't know, I think it's just habit," she said honestly. She wasn't used to interviewing kids and hearing all of these honest and simple questions. "But I also want to remind people watching who you are. Maybe they just joined the show at this point."

"Oh. It's kinda weird."

"Yeah, I guess it's kinda weird."

"But Lu?"

"Yeah, Miss Cumberbun?"

"Ooh, you got it?"

"Got what?"

"My name."

Lu smiled.

"Where is the next adventure going to take place?" she asked but didn't wait for an answer. "I mean, the moon, some castle. Maybe even in Austria? Or far away?"

"What about right here?" Lu said and again turned to look at her, but glanced at her face and then turned back towards the school.

"Right here?"

"Yeah, right here, right now. This could be where it all starts. Maybe the next story starts right here and right now and maybe you're part of it," Lu said with little emotion and seemed even in a way detached from what he was saying. He was excited about a kid not following the rules, but when it came to the next phase of his life and adventure, it was almost as if it was fate and he just relayed the information he was given.

Meghan blushed and even brought her hand up to her face and looked at the cameraman with a combination of 'Isn't this exciting?' and 'Me? Little old me?' all in one glance and a few movements of her hands. The cameraman enjoyed the whole show of her innocence and clear affection for the young boy she was interviewing.

"Do you mean that maybe I'm in the story, too, Lu?"

"Sure, why not?"

"Oh, that's so exciting. So maybe the next story begins right here and right now, just like you said, in, wait, what's this town called again?"

"You don't know the town you're in?"

"We flew in yesterday from the States," she said with pride and fatigue.

"You didn't happen to bring any Reese's, did you?"

"Any what?"

"Reese's. It's a candy, but it has chocolate and peanut butter."

"I know Reese's."

"Oh good. But did you bring any?"

"Uh, no, I didn't."

"That's too bad," Lu said. "That's one thing I miss here in Holland--Reese's. My dad said that you could find them in this one shop in Utrecht," Lu turned towards her again. "That's nearby. Just on the train. I'd say it's worth going just for the Reese's, but it would be easier if you just brought a whole bunch from the States, then we'd have them right now."

"That's true, that would have been nice."

"Maybe next time?"

"Maybe next time, Lu."

"Miss Cumberbon?"

"Cumberbun."

"Cumberbun."

"Yes?"

"I kinda have to go," Lu stood up. "School's over now and everyone is gone and I have to turn in my sheet with everyone I wrote up."

"Oh, OK," Meghan said, not quite used to not being the one who decided when the interview was over, but it seemed like it was over. She wasn't quite ready to let him go just yet, though.

"Lu?"

"Yeah," he answered, half turning towards her and half looking towards the school where he had to turn in his sheet. She had a big question, but wasn't sure if she dared to ask it. She hesitated. He was hankering to leave. She had one shot. The kid clearly had things to do. She couldn't do it. She fell back to mindless banter questions and avoided what was now eating her up inside.

"How many kids did you write up?" she gave in and realized she had been tense when she exhaled a little stronger than she expected.

"Drie," Lu said looking at his sheet.

"How many?"

"Drie," Lu said again.

"What does that mean?"

"Here's your first Dutch lesson. It means three."

"Dree," Meghan said.

"Good job," Lu said and put his fist out waiting for a fist bump. She obliged.

"Oh, and Driehoek," Lu said.

"Driehoek?" Meghan repeated.

"You asked the name of the town. It means three corners or triangle."

She nodded and he was about to leave. She had one last shot.

"Lu?" she asked as he had taken a step away. He turned back towards her.

"When does the next adventure start?" she asked, both wanting to know and fearful of being involved.

He came a step towards her, looked at her in the eyes and said without any signs of personal involvement but in just a few words that would change the life of dear Miss Cumberbun forever. He leaned in close. He whispered.

"It just did."

2

OH NO. NOT AGAIN.

HISTORY REPEATS ITSELF. KINDA.

"Only a life lived for others is a life worthwhile."

— ALBERT EINSTEIN

"Where did Pepper go?" Lu asked quietly with a tinge of trepidation in his voice.

"He's probably pooping," Li said, always one to bring in the basics in case they're ever lacking.

"He'll catch up," Charlie said as he kept walking straight ahead on the path. The trees walled them in and covered them from above. Autumn was all around them in bursts of red nestled in a cozy ocean of oranges and yellow that lined the floor of the woods in the center of The Netherlands.

They walked a bit further without saying anything. Usually, Pepper caught up with them and then, for reasons they talked about extensively but never got a reasonable answer for, he would run full speed at them from behind, catch up to them easily, but then continue on another ten or twenty meters as if to show that, who knows, maybe just that he could, that he was OK, that he was the leader of the pack.

Lu looked behind him, but kept his mouth closed.

Even Li turned around.

Charlie kept walking. He knew they'd all be alright.

Another five minutes, which is somewhere near an eternity when someone you love isn't with you and you don't know where they are.

Something struck Charlie in his heart. Almost as if something thin and sharp, but easy to find in the forest, like the stem of a leaf. He flinched, stopped, and turned around.

Still too proud to say anything, always too sure that things would always be OK, he kept quiet but did look over the heads of his two sons back along the path from which they came.

No sprinting black animal. No dog that was, if there was a range from a zero of suicidal and a ten was giddy with joy, prancing around the clouds at a level twelve where there was nothing amiss with the universe. The people he loved, the paths to rocket down, the frogs to kiss, foxes to visit in the holes, and no coyotes like they had back in San Francisco.

San Francisco held many memories for the boys: burritos in the Mission, In-N-Out Burger visits were a spiritual rebirth every single time. But there was one afternoon that none of the three of them would ever forget.

It all had ended well, but it was a test, a scare, maybe even a step along the path from boyhood to manhood. Nothing had been the same since. Their lives had been transformed by the secret that they all held in their hearts and minds since that afternoon back in the city of their birth.

The three of them stood on the trail together, shoulder to shoulder. The boys had grown up quite a bit in the couple of years since that fateful afternoon in The City. They rarely uttered the words since that time and it almost became a joke like the wizard in Harry Potter that no one dared utter the name of.

There was something about secrets that made them spooky and scary and, when you're a young pre-teen boy, they carry a lot of weight and although it might mean not telling your friends about what happened long ago, you somehow manage to raise your own standard of respect and keep that secret as much effort as that takes.

Lu and Li and Charlie were all thinking the same thing. If there were some sort of thought-o-meter that could measure what was above their heads, it would all be the same color or measure the same vibrational rating because they were all thinking the exact same thing.

In the seconds that passed since they all turned around, no one dared say a word as they only hoped that their beloved dog would come shooting out from under a brush or around that last bend or at this point they would even have been OK with him falling from one of the trees above.

No one wanted to say anything, but they all thought it. Only a few birds chirped. The breeze came through the trees and made a sound they hadn't heard before, sounds you don't notice if you're walking or talking.

It was possible that none of them was breathing. They

were all listening. A lie detector would have proven that they were all thinking the same exact thing and even down to the two words that they each had on the tip of their tongues.

Had this been a set in Hollywood, complete with leaves falling at just the right time and the colors all so bright that it was almost too perfect, they might have all said the two words at exactly the same time and after a slow fade of the camera to black and it would have been the opening scene of the movie.

But this wasn't Hollywood. This was Driehoek. A small village in the woodsy middle of the Kingdom of The Netherlands.

It came from the one of the three who possibly had the deepest love for the black pooch. He didn't give it any good stage drama, no whispering, no special effects. He just said the words but the effect it had on the three of them needed no introduction and only produced adrenaline and fear for the near future.

Li said the words that the others were thinking. He didn't want to say them because he didn't want to believe them. If he said them they might come true. He didn't want to relive any of that afternoon.

But he couldn't hold back. It was as if another part of himself said the words. Maybe not his mind or even his lips, as if his throat or the vocal cords weren't his own as he was the one who wanted to be drawn back to the past the least of the three. But the words escaped his lips.

"Kite Hill."

3

BREAKING NEWS

BUT ISN'T NO NEWS GOOD NEWS?

"You can never solve a problem on the level on which it was created."

— ALBERT EINSTEIN

"We did everything we could," Charlotte said with a sniffle and dropped down heavily onto the sofa.

Li snuggled into the crook of her arm which, although he was now taller than his mother, was still one of the sweetest feelings in the history of sweetest things for a parent. He sniffled and tried to hold back his tears, but they just flowed down his cheeks.

"Ach, liefje," Charlotte held his head in her hands and kissed the top of his head. If there was any silver lining in a tragedy, it was the joy of providing and showering love on those who most needed it.

"He was right behind us," Lu said and sniffed, keeping, literally, a stiff upper lip.

"We've done everything we could," Charlie said, trying to put a logical, rational spin on the situation. It wasn't working. "The whole neighborhood came together and we scoured that forest with flashlights and every kid yelling out Pepper's name. We did everything we could. We can't say we didn't try."

"But we still don't have him," Li's words were caught up in the phlegm of misery. "I don't care how much we did, we didn't do enough."

"Let's get our minds off of it," Charlotte said and turned up the volume on the TV.

"I can't get my mind off it," Lu screamed. "That's the worst advice I've ever heard," he said through tears and ended up in a coughing fit.

He went into the other warm armpit of his mother and the four of them sat lined up like ducklings on the sofa and pretended to watch the screen in front of them.

For once, the two parents were relieved that a screen was taking over the attention of the kids--and even the parents.

The blue glow swarmed them and enveloped them in a blanket of thick distraction. The news brought mayhem and chaos elsewhere on the planet but none of it compared to the emptiness in young boys' hearts when their dog is gone.

The sniffles slowed and silence overtook the family and the love poured out from the windows just as did the flickering rays of the screen.

The weather forecaster had a few seconds to give a preview of her later full report, but shared the news that the night sky was so clear that it was worth stepping outside and enjoying as the clarity in a densely populated and brightly lit country like The Netherlands was a rarity.

What was also strange, according the newscaster who seemed terribly excited about it all, was that the moon was also full but still the stars were more visible than usual. The combination of the lack of clouds, the full moon, and the bright stars were something that seemed like it was worth waiting for her full forecast later in the program.

The family sitting on the couch outside the forest looked like zombies with glazed eyes. It wasn't clear if they were taking in anything the talking heads on the screen said, but it probably got into their minds at least subconsciously as their thoughts and dreams were full of a little furry face that looked up at them and asked without any single word: are we going on a walk now?

Any of them would have given anything to have that little dog back asking for a walk in the woods.

They were silent as different people gave the news of the day. Something in the local political world about a coalition of parties trying to work together. Li's translation in his own mind was a coalition of neighbors working together towards a successful outcome.

There was an empty spot on the couch where Pepper often watched the news together with his family. It was empty not only in the physical sense, but there was a hole there among the blankets and pillows that had the effect of a black hole in space that pulls everything into it and it all disappears. The love and sadness in that living room was being sucked into the vortex of Pepper's pillow at an alarming rate. Something had to give or their hearts would be emptied by the end of the evening.

As if the television network had a direct line into the sadness of the room, the next segment of the news could not have had a more powerful effect on the melancholy of the room. Except that it was going to take it a notch deeper into oblivion.

"An uplifting story today from the dog shelter in Gouda," the news anchor said, papers in her hand and a large photo of a happy dog behind her.

"Oh great," Charlotte said.

"Just turn it off, I can't handle it," Li said.

"Turn it up," Charlie dropped the words into the air.

"What's that word when you like torturing yourself, dad?"

"Let's just watch," Charlie said calmly and turned up the volume.

"After our call out last week to our viewers asking if there were happy homes where these dogs could come live instead of being put to sleep, we received an overwhelming response of love and care from our community," she said, smiling and happy at a level only dogs can bring to people.

"Do you see Pepper in there?" Lu asked, moving up to the edge of the sofa.

"It was probably filmed last week or something," Li said and sniffled again.

"Shh, let's just watch," Charlotte put her finger to her lips to listen.

The screen was filled with yapping and jumping and just-way-too-happy dogs of all sizes and sorts while kids and families stood around them and hugged and parents put their arms around their kids because they were proud and so happy for the children.

"OK, I get it, they're happy," Lu started with a big snif-fle. "But for us, right now, this is like a horror movie."

"Do we have to watch this?" Li asked.

"I guess not," Charlotte reached for the remote to turn it all off and make it all just go away. There had been enough trials and tribulations for the day. Pepper was her choice, her name, and her baby. The whole sons and husbands thing was great, but Pepper was her true love.

"No, keep it on," Lu said, much more decisive than his usual I-don't-even-know-if-I-have-shoes-on self.

"Whatever," Charlotte got up with the power that only a mother has when she has to dig into the reserves to resurrect her family from the depths of loss. "Who wants hot chocolate?"

No one answered.

"I'm going to make us hot chocolate," she left the living room.

Finally, after painful minutes of really annoying happy people with dogs wiggling and clearly overly joyous, it finally switched to something much more appropriate: the traffic news.

Things had been clogged up on the highways of Holland. It was getting colder and they suggested winter tires pretty soon.

"In what would have normally been just a regular story of a traffic accident," the newscaster began in Dutch. "It turned into something of a, well, I don't know, some might call it a miracle," she paused and turned to the screen where a reporter came on. "Iris, tell us what you see out there on the roads."

Iris, the reporter in the dark, stood on the side of a

road and lifted her microphone. She was soaking wet. It wasn't raining.

"The news crew and I were heading back to the station tonight but the highways were pretty full, so we took the smaller side roads."

"We were on a narrow road and, now that it's autumn, it was already quite dark, but of course we had our lights on," Iris said as if she had all day to tell her personal story of driving back to the news station.

The anchor in the studio, aware that they didn't have time for a full feature on Iris's driving habits, hurried her up a bit. "Tell us what happened, Iris."

"Well, I don't quite know how to explain this," Iris started and the camera switched back, possibly unintentionally, to the studio where the anchor checked her watch and motioned with her hand to hurry it up.

"But there's a full moon out, but it was low in the sky. I don't know if I've ever really seen it that low," she said.

Back to the anchor. She had the patience of a nun, but a nun who had a show to run. This was live, prime time TV after all. She said nothing so as not to interrupt the flow. But her face was clearing saying *'This better be good or Iris is going to be working the rising water level documentary by the time she's back to the station.'*

"It was even almost blinding," she said again way too slowly. "But then there was a street lamp in front of us to the right and finally a third light came from off the side of the road to the left," she paused every so slightly. "It was a perfect triangle."

The anchor was about to cut her off just as her earpiece was humming with a louder and louder program director who was getting antsy. They needed to shut this down.

"Iris?" the anchor tried to intervene.

Iris just kept going, seemingly completely unaware that she was on live TV and more like she was explaining a story to her friends later at the bar—which she would probably also do later.

Charlotte came back into the living room with a tray of four hot chocolates and announced, "OK, who wants hot chocolate?"

Three mouths shouted as loudly and as quickly as they could a chorus of, "Shhhhh!"

Charlotte did a little head shake as if to say 'Geez, sorry for bringing a little joy and love to the room.' She did the smart thing and sat down and watched the news.

"Who's this?" she asked.

"Shhhhhhhhh!" it all came again but this time even more quick and forceful. Charlotte zipped it.

"That third light," Iris pointed behind her where no one watching could possibly see. "It blinked a couple of times, then went out, then came back on," she just kept going. "I didn't think much of it, but as we got closer, I thought I saw something like a face that the little light illuminated."

She took a deep breath but didn't leave any time for anyone to interrupt her. At this point, the only thing that was going to stop her was the station shutting down the feed, which they were seconds away from doing.

"It was a person," Iris said in something of a whisper. Even the anchor, who was briefly back on screen, leaned in closer. She took out her earpiece. The screen went back to Iris.

"But off the road was a ditch, a canal, or at least some water," Iris again in quick breaths as she started to hurry her story. Which was a good idea for many reasons.

"We drove up to where I had seen the light but it was now extinguished. As we pulled up, I saw it one last time and realized what was going on," Iris was now telling her story from another place, as if the words were coming to her and she was just telling it like it happened exactly.

"There was a car in the water and it was upside down," she said. "I saw one more flicker of light and, I wish I could get this image out of my mind as it was horrifying but that last glimmer of light was a woman's face and she was in the car that was upside down and about to go under the water."

No one in the studio, no one in the living room, no one in the country who was watching, moved or took a breath. The stillness of the night stopped time waiting on Iris's next words who had single-handedly transformed an evening traffic report into something of a horror movie.

"We jumped out of the truck and the three of us dove into the water," Iris was no longer breathing or blinking, just talking.

"Mark, our cameraman, and I were underwater and we could see that tiny light that was probably her cellphone. We pulled and pulled at the door handle but it wouldn't open. I didn't have much breath left, but we both it gave it all of our might and it gave. The door opened." The entire nation exhaled.

"Water rushed in and the woman couldn't swim away.

Mark and I grabbed her and the three of us struggled and tugged and tore and kicked and it finally all gave way and she was free."

Iris took a breath. "We pulled her up and out and to the surface and over to the edge. She was alive."

"We asked her if she was OK, but she couldn't speak. She was certainly in shock. But the strange thing was that she just kept saying this one word, over and over," Iris had no concept of time or where she was. The story was just telling itself. It just happened to be coming out of her mouth.

"It turns out, she's not Dutch and was here doing an interview, but she kept saying that one word, like she was in a trance. She finally told us it was the only word she knew in Dutch and she had just learned from a kid she was interviewing today. She said 'Drie.'"

Lu whispered to no one and no one heard it, "That's me, Miss Cumberbun."

Iris rattled her story out as if she just had to get the words from her body. "Then she said another word and later she told us that she didn't know what the word meant but for some reason she just said it. She said 'Hoek.'"

Iris stopped and just stared into the camera. The cameraman didn't know quite what to do. The anchor was frozen in her studio.

It was terribly unprofessional, but Iris started crying. Not a big weepy snotty adventure but more that tears started streaming down her cheeks as if her eyes opened up the spouts and it just rolled out.

"Driehoek," was the last word that Iris said before the screen went back to the studio and the anchor got her act together and brought things back to the weather, that full moon, and what was certainly an abbreviated version of the closing out of the news.

Driehoek. *Triangle*.

Back in the living room, Lu's body was tingling with more pins and needles than exist in a yarn warehouse.

As if the rest of the family sensed that Lu had something going on, they all looked at him. His eyes were full of tears but his face was stoic.

Lu, usually the playful joker who took next-to-nothing seriously said in such an ominous tone that no one in the room recognized the voice.

Lu said simply, "I know where Pepper is."

4

DRIEHOEK

TRIANGLE

"Try not to become a man of success, but rather try to become a man of value."

— ALBERT EINSTEIN

"W hat do you mean you know where Pepper is?" Li asked, but Lu wasn't waiting around for an answer. He was already on his way out of the living room at speeds not seen in the 11-year-old since the first time they realized that the pizza could be delivered to the front door in their little town.

"Hey! Where are you going?" Charlotte yelled from the living room, but no one answered.

The three laggards decided to stop yelling and questioning but to get up and follow Lu.

He was already in the foyer putting on his shoes. Usually, this took a decree of government to even get him near his shoes much less some with laces and then to put one on each foot and lace them.

"Get a flashlight," he commanded in a tone unlike the personality of the boy who wanted to read just one more chapter even though he was already five minutes late for school. "And shoes," his voice wasn't quite normal. "And hurry."

"Lu," Charlie asked. "Where are we going?"

"To get Pepper."

None of them needed to ask any more questions. They all put on their shoes almost as fast as their young leader, grabbed light jackets and flashlights.

He would have gone without them, but he needed them to help triangulate. He didn't know the word triangulate, but he knew instinctively that he needed them and to do that.

"Ready?" said the boy who was first in line only if the line was for hot fries with mayonnaise.

"Ready," his brother said in a rare show of support. But this wasn't PS4, this wasn't school, this wasn't friends or basketball. In fact, this wasn't world domination, this wasn't the extinction of the human species, this wasn't even a Reese's delivery truck.

This was bigger.

This was important. This was pure and unconditional love the likes of which exist within our atmosphere, sometimes just outside of it, but exists in full bloom and is only suppressed as we smother it with blankets of anxiety and worry and doubt.

This was beyond brotherhood. This was beyond family. This was a single, solitary, and all-powerful love that the boys only knew for one living and breathing being on the surface of the earth. This was Pepper.

Shoes on, jackets on, flashlights on. No words. Lu looked at each of them but said nothing. This from the boy whose car companions requested a white noise app on the car stereo. He just looked at his family, felt sure they were ready, turned, opened the gate and did something he also rarely did. He ran.

Realizing quickly that yelling things such as 'Hey! Where are you going?' or maybe 'Wait up!' or even 'Have you lost your brain?' were all pointless as Lu wasn't even waiting up. They ran.

To the right, first left, one block and they were at the edge of the forest. The three of them caught up with Lu. He yet again said nothing. Just the fact that he was without words was cause enough for concern that they didn't question it.

Again he turned and ran.

The moon was bright and the flashlights only lighted the close path in front of them. They turned them off and their eyes adjusted to the darkness of the night and the ray of the full moon.

Left into the depths of the forest. Li couldn't hold back any longer. He had to say something, he had to ask, he had to at least doubt his younger brother. This had gone on too long that little brother was running the show.

"Do you know where you're going?"

So out of character that a fingerprint verification wouldn't have been out of line, Lu again didn't speak but just nodded.

"Why don't you talk?" Li was annoyed and felt much more at home that he could again be annoyed with his brother. It also, at least temporarily, took his mind off of their lost dog.

Lu knew something that the others didn't and it wasn't so much that he was relishing that fact, but more that he wanted to stay focused. Maybe speaking would hinder his focus. The others could only guess what was going on inside of his head--or just outside of it.

He smiled. If you didn't know what was in his head and if you didn't know what he knew, then, yep, it was certainly annoying. But on the other hand, if he knew what the others needed to know and they had to let this sly smile exist and not question it in order to accomplish their mission? It was worth it all.

Lu looked up into the dark night sky. As if he had been an astronomer and knew where stars were or how to see which were where and how to find the north through this star or calculate where that was through that star, he was reading the sky.

No one dared interrupt again although they all wanted to.

He looked at them again as if taking roll call. They were all there. It wasn't such a high number to count: three. Drie. Driehoek.

He looked up and then, as if he was following a moon ray with his eyes and his head, he looked from the top of the sky to the top of the atmosphere to the top of the trees to a clump of trees where there was no trail. He went that way. His family followed.

Through the bushes and between the trees, over the roots and weaving in and out of what seemed like twigs that were sprouting from everywhere, Lu knew exactly where he was going. The others followed silently.

They got to a clearing in the forest. There were sand dunes in what was an oasis from the deep and dark forest. The moonlight lit it all up as if there were floodlights along the perimeter.

In one corner of the dunes was a lamp post. Under it a little plaque that said something about the name of the forest they were in. Lu looked to it then looked to the other side of the open space but there was no light anywhere else.

"Driehoek," Lu said.

"Driehoek?" Li mimicked, happy to question his brother's sanity at every opportunity.

"Driehoek," Charlotte said as if wanting to roll the word around in her mouth.

5

BRO

STAY IN SCHOOL. NO, SERIOUSLY.

"Education is what remains after one has forgotten what one has learned in school."

— ALBERT EINSTEIN

Li again couldn't handle the suspense. "Lu, you said you knew where Pepper was," he looked to mom and dad to remind himself that he should try to be at least a little civil. "So, where is he?"

"See that light?" Lu asked and pointed to the lamp post that everyone could clearly see.

"We see it," Charlie said not wanting to interrupt or delay.

"See the moon?" Lu said.

"Duh," Li said, which was 21st century 14-year-old barbarian dialect for 'Yes, we do.'

"We need the third light to make the triangle," Lu said in a tone that was so convincing even Li wasn't going to question it—which was maybe the second or third miracle of the evening.

They all looked around.

"But that could be anywhere," Charlotte said.

"Well," Li said, all inhibitions aside for the briefest black holes in the time space dimension where he was allowed to say something that showed that maybe he knew something and even though it was extremely uncool to admit it, this was an emergency.

The words escaped his lips and he would forever have to live up to their power. He asked, "What kind of triangle is it?"

Lu was still looking around the dunes for a sign of a third light. Mother and father of said 14-year-old boy human specimen were staring at him as if he were in a museum. Charlie's vision went so far as to see the inscription on the informational plaque under the species: '*Contrary to popular belief at the time, the 14-year-old male, corpus teenitus, has actual brain function equal to seven times that was originally studied in the living species at the time.*'

"I'm sorry," Charlie just couldn't help it. Dog be gone, this was galaxy shattering. "Did you just ask what type of triangle it was?"

Although Li's gut told him to fight back and keep his role as master of all teenager mindless blobs of blood and guts and bones and video game thumbs, his heart had one word for his dad.

"Yes."

Lu missed the entire trans-species exchange and was back to business.

"What do you mean, what kind of triangle is it?"

"Well, there's the pythagorean theorem," Li started and as he said it he noticed his dad staggering to his right as he seemed to be losing his balance.

In reality, his dad was speaking directly with heaven and thanking the gods and making a quick side deal that all bets were off and all of his prayers had been answered and the entire rest of his existence on the planet was just plain dessert.

Li only saw his dad swaying a little bit but kept going. "That theorem says that, if one angle of the triangle is a right angle—"

"Bro, are you seriously talking geometry?" Lu interrupted.

"Do you want to find Pepper?" Li shot back in snap.

"Yes."

"Then listen for a change," Li said and both parents were relieved that the boys that had been previously been known as Li and Lu had not been abducted but were alive and well in the forest.

"If one angle of the triangle is a right angle and we know the lengths of two sides of the triangle then we can find out the length of the other side."

"Bro," Lu was feeling way back to little brother self. "Totally awesome but what are you talking about?"

"The lamp post is one light, maybe the moon is the other light, where's the third light?"

They all looked around but there was just the lamp post.

"We have the flashlights," Charlotte said.

"But the moon is so far away," Li thought aloud.

"Maybe it's all wrong," Charlie said and regretted it before even the last word exited his mind.

"I just want to find Pepper," Charlotte let loose with what she was truly feeling.

"We need to combine what we have," Lu said, again surpassing his age in oddly wise comments.

"The science, the math," Li said, again proof that alien beings could inject intelligence into human life forms, even if temporarily.

"Add in the magic," Lu said.

"What magic?" Charlotte asked.

"My magic," Lu said, again just out-of-place convincing. Charlotte was immediately convinced although she had no logical reason to be.

"We need to make a triangle," Li said.

"Maybe it's not the moon itself," Charlie said.

"Maybe it's a place where we can see the moon," Charlotte added.

"Or a place where the moon is reflected," Lu said and looked towards the middle of the dunes.

In the brush and bushes and trees, there was an oasis within the oasis of green. Inside of that island of green encircled by the ocean of sand was a pond. Without further ado, they walked that way.

From the water, if they stood back and up on the incline of the sand dune, they could see both the reflection of the moon and the light from the lamp post.

"I still don't know where the third light source is," Lu wondered aloud.

Letters and math spilled out from a place in Li's mind that was usually reserved to Tuesdays between one and two-thirty in the afternoon. "A squared plus B squared is C squared," he started and kept going before any snarky commentary might be floated his way. "If we know how far it is from the water to the lamp post and then we measure that same distance in another direction, then we can figure out how long the third side is."

Convinced without a shred of doubt now that other ethereal beings could take over the minds of young boys, it was no longer of any use to make comments on the topic and Charlie turned to logic.

"Li," he looked at his son. "How many steps from the water to the lamp?"

Li didn't need to be asked twice. He started walking and counting aloud.

"Dad?" Lu asked.

"Lu, just a sec," Charlie kept his eyes on Li.

"Dad?" Lu again, but again Charlie focused on Li's steps, trying to keep a little bit of a count to himself. Maybe 50 by now.

"What's that?" Lu asked and pointed.

"What's what, liefje?" Charlotte looked to where Lu was pointing.

"That," Lu said and started walking away.

"Lu?" Charlotte started but had learned earlier that following instead of talking was working out pretty well for the evening so far. She followed him. Soon, she saw what he was looking at.

Lu and Charlotte walked out away from Charlie to another side of the sand dune oasis in the middle of the forest as Li counted his steps from the water to the lamp post.

6

WE HAVE THE KNOWLEDGE. IT'S JUST A LITTLE BURIED SOMETIMES.

MATH TO THE RESCUE. AGAIN.

"Pure mathematics is, in its way, the poetry of logical ideas."

— ALBERT EINSTEIN

"It's about 50 steps," Li said as he came back. "Where did Lu and mom go?"

"Over there," Charlie pointed. As he pointed, he finally saw it too.

"Watch this, dad," Li said and with the pride of a son who could show his father that he actually knew something, counted his steps out loud. In a sign that they were adapting to their new home country, Li counted in Dutch. "Een, twee, drie," and headed towards his brother and mother.

If there was a light source that was not measured by lumens but purely by energy, it came out of the heart of that boy as he felt he was part of the solution and the light rays that radiated out from him into the dark skies above could only be one thing: pride.

Dog or no dog, there was power in the light of the night.

"About forty," Li screamed back to his dad. Charlie made his way to where they all were.

"It's like there's glass in this tree," Charlotte said and got out of the way to show her husband.

"See it, dad?" Lu said? "It's like sap."

"But it's sort of solid now, so it reflects like glass," Li said.

"We have three points of the triangle," Charlie said.

"But what does it mean?" Charlotte asked.

"I don't know," Charlie again spoke what was on his mind before he thought.

"From the lamp to the water is 50 steps," Li said. "And then from the water to this tree is 40 steps," he paused. "So, what's 50 times 50?"

"Two thousand five hundred," Lu answered before anyone could pull out a phone.

"Then 40 times 40?" Charlotte asked.

Li looked up, Lu looked the other way.

"One thousand six hundred," they said at almost the same time.

"What's two thousand five hundred plus one thousand six hundred?" Li asked but before he could do the calculation in his head and, granted, he was the one who asked the question and spent that possible solution finding time in asking, Lu answered.

"Four thousand one hundred," Lu said.

"So A squared plus B squared is C squared," but Li then looked confused. "Which one is the right angle?"

"Uh," Charlotte dropped in with a splash of hesitation. "Can't we just walk the distance from the tree to the lamp?"

"Oh," Charlie said.

"I guess so," Lu added.

Li started walking. They all waited.

"About 60," he yelled back.

"But what does it tell us?" Charlotte asked.

"I don't know," Charlie wished he wasn't the only one who always said that.

Li came back. "But we know the lengths of the sides. What do we need to figure out?"

"Maybe the whole triangle thing is wrong," Lu said.

"I don't think so," Charlotte said with more conviction than she could back up rationally.

"We're just missing something," Charlie said.

"Yeah," Li said. "We're missing Pepper."

"Maybe he's in the middle of the triangle?" Lu said and looked to where that would be. "Let's go there."

They walked, Lu jogged, to the place that was about the center of the triangle of the lamp, the water, and the shining tree sap.

"One of the points is wrong," Li said with more assertion than ever.

"How do you know?" Lu said.

"How do you know it's not?"

"Good point," Lu said on his way to joining the debate team.

If there exists a god of mathematics, he dropped yet

another lightning bolt of wisdom into his star of the night and Li asked a question, but it was more that he was asking for confirmation.

"It's 50 steps from the lamp to the water and it's 40 steps from the tree to the water. We said that was then 2,500 and 1,600 which would be, uh, how much Lu?"

"Four thousand one hundred," Lu said in a flash.

"Right," Li kept going. "So what did we say was the square root of 4,100?"

"We didn't," Charlotte said.

"What times what is about 41?" Charlie asked, always open to math quizzes.

"Nothing," Lu said. "Well, nothing exactly."

"We don't need exact," Li said, "we just need a good guess." For possibly the first time in the history of teenage mankind, he understood the importance of getting the bigger picture in mathematics.

"Six times six is thirty-six," Charlotte said.

"Seven times seven is forty-nine," Lu said.

"So, something between sixty and seventy," Li said.

"But we know that," Charlotte said. "That brings us to the water."

"I can see it in my head," Li said and for yet another first in his fourteen years of existence, he did see it in his head. "But we're opposite."

"Huh?" Lu grunted.

"Or, well, turned over," Li couldn't get it out. "We need to flip it over."

"It's not the water," Lu said.

"It's not the water," Li agreed.

"Mom," Li directed. "You go to the lamp post and walk

about 40 steps but at the other angle from the one towards water."

"But that's into the middle of the forest," she said.

"Please?"

She didn't say anything. She started walking towards the lamp post.

"Dad?" Li asked and although Charlie was churning numbers and angles in his head, he didn't see it clearly. He needed Li's instructions. "From right here, from the reflection in the moon to the sap, you're going to walk about 50 steps that way," and he pointed directly into the deep and dark forest.

"OK," he succumbed and was going to do pretty much whatever either of his sons had in mind at this point.

"Lu," Li said. "Let's go," and they walked together towards the water.

When they got there, Li looked at the lamp post and at the glistening sap tree. He looked into the forest where he sent his parents.

"What do you see, Lu?" Li asked and Lu didn't need the question a second time.

"Pepper," Lu said.

"Good," Li said. "Let's go."

From the water, they walked at a ninety-degree angle from the intersection of the middle point of the tree and lamp towards the center of the forest.

7

IT TAKES A VILLAGE

OR A FAMILY

"Information is not knowledge."

— ALBERT EINSTEIN

They didn't need a flashlight on the glowing sand floor of the dunes, but once they got into the forest it was pitch black.

"Don't turn on the flashlight," Lu said and, for reasons unknown to this day, his brother agreed without pushback.

Rays of moonlight streaked through the trees above and lit up the forest floor as if there were dimmer halogen spotlights sprinkled throughout the canopy above. It was enough to make out the silhouettes although this part of the forest was dense with roots and brush and it was slow going.

They kept their path straight and only stopped when they heard a noise. Once it was a branch breaking and they saw their dad ahead and to the right.

They heard something of a howl and they were pretty

sure it wasn't a fox. Up to the left was their mother who had just tripped and fell and yelped.

If they kept going straight the four of them were going to meet up in a matter of minutes.

Li would later never admit this, but he tried to calculate the distance from that middle point of the longest side to the right angle ahead, and although he couldn't quite figure it out, he knew it had something to do with two right angles and then splitting up the large triangle into two smaller ones and where they were heading was the point where the two smaller triangles and the larger one met.

There were some grunts and huffs and puffs, a bit of brushing off leaves or who-knew-what from jeans and shoes. The four of them met at this middle point somewhere deep in the forest and Li suddenly had a vision that they were here for nothing. He said nothing, but they were all looking to him.

No one wanted to speak first. A jumping dog would have been a nice distraction from the silence. Maybe a little yelping and biting and excitement. It would have broken the absolute stillness. The forest floor acted like sound insulation and it seemed that even the breaths of the four people weren't audible.

Charlie lowered his body to the ground. He put one knee on the carpet of dark and moist green. He put his palm to the earth. He closed his eyes. No one knew what else to do so they just stood still.

It wasn't so much that he could see something like a map in the roots and twigs and vines, but through his hand came a connection with a long and solitary vine that lit up from his hand and traveled between Li and Lu and off into the forest behind the boys.

He wasn't about to explain to his family that he could see this vine light up on the ground, but this was an emergency. Lu had seen the triangle. Li had received some sort of download from a god of geometry. It was his turn. It wasn't yet time to tell his family what he was doing. Not just yet.

But it was time to lock in.

Although he had his eyes closed he clearly felt the single vine go from his fingers through the two boys and he stood and followed it.

Not daring to stop him, the family stayed silent and followed him as he parted his sons apparently looking like he knew what he was doing or where he was going.

Only a handful of steps from where they were standing was a clump of brush and leaves and a larger fallen tree branch.

Charlie's feeling of the vine lessened and his senses turned auditory. The silence was deafening. He only heard the breaths of his family. The quicker pulse of his son's breath. The hurried but soft in and out of his concerned wife. Lu's breath was slow, but had the occasional sniffle.

There was another breath. It was slow and labored. But clear. Charlie had his eyes open but wasn't seeing. He recounted the breaths: Li, Charlotte, Lu, and even his own. He turned those off as if there were a filter or check boxes that he unchecked.

Just the one breath left. It was weak. It was tired. But it was there.

It was right under them. He looked down. There was

nothing to see. There were only branches, only leaves, twigs, brush. Forest stuff.

Charlotte fell to her knees and started sobbing.

"Mama, wat is er?" Lu fell to his knees and put his arm around his mother. Mama, what is it?

She reached her hands into the brush as if assisting the birth of a large mammal. She knew where to put her hands. No one said a thing. They only watched.

She sobbed and sniffled. It was the only sound in the entire forest.

She reached deeper under the brush. She leaned in. She groped. She grasped. She was lifting and then she pulled.

A wet and dark animal was in her hands. It was still. Lu gasped.

With that noise, the animal twitched and opened a dark eye up towards them. In the deep and dark forest there was only a single light and it came from the glimmer of the eye of the animal reflecting the ray of moonlight.

Only Li managed to get out a word past the heart that was up in his throat so far he wasn't sure he could breathe. But that one word slipped into the silence. A word wrapped in desperation and rasp.

"Pepper."

EPILOGUE

"They grow up so fast!"
Dear Reader,
I must share with you one of the reasons I write these stories down.

TIME CAPSULE.

We will only have today, well, today. When today becomes tomorrow then we call it yesterday. It's no longer today.

While I don't need to hold onto the past, I do enjoy documenting it.

Part of this comes from a time when my mother read aloud letters to me and my sister as we took trains through Europe. They were terribly boring and long and mostly talked about the price of grain and corn and other farm talk.

But it was a slice of history.

It was frozen in time.

I already look back at The Secret of Kite Hill and

think, "Oh, they were so cute and lovable! Where did those boys go!?"

HOW ARE YOU DOCUMENTING YOUR LIFE?

Do you write down any stories? Remember, it's not to win literary awards and it may not even be that someone is going to read them back to kids at some point.

The "documentation" or telling of stories helps to cement them into our minds, our memories, and, dare I say, into our hearts.

From there, they can grow and blossom and they might sprout a new memory or wrap around someone's heart and hold on and then you have a made a *connection*.

Is there more to life than connection?

It's all we really need. Food, water, and connection.

Write down your stories. Better yet, record a few minutes talking into your phone. It doesn't have to be the big stuff. Go for the little things. What did your aunt say that was so funny last night? Your neighbor and his silly habit?

Tell your story.

Bradley Charbonneau
Driebergen, The Netherlands

RELATIONSHIP

Building a relationship with my readers is one of the best things about writing. (Another one is getting lost in my fictional characters!)

I truly want to know if you can feel something in Lu and/or Lu that you have in you.

- Do they resonate with you?
- Do you have a favorite? Why?
- What would you like to know about him?
- What other questions might you have?

Are you interested in seeing where Li & Lu might head to next? Would you like to be first in line to experience stories *before* they're even in the production line?

I'm looking to build out my "Advance Reader Team." It's a small group of readers who would like to get their hands on my work before it's available to the public.

In return, all I ask is for any comments on spelling mistakes, grammar questions, and most of all, if there are plot lines that you don't understand or need more explanation about.

I also occasionally send an email with details about **new books**, **sneak peeks** into Works In Progress, early bird **deals**, as well as exclusive, **Readers Only insights** into the writing and publishing process.

If you'd like to sign up to be on the Advanced Reader Team and/or the Readers Only mailing list, just click on this link and let me know which email to send to. Thank you!

Join Bradley Charbonneau's Team [https://goo.gl/KmH9NL]

ABOUT THE AUTHOR

Bradley Charbonneau used to call himself "a travel writer who didn't travel or write." It was funny. Until it was no longer funny.

He wasn't doing two things he loved dearly.

Through some drastic measures, he has changed that. If you'd like to read about that journey, it's documented in his book "Every Single Day" where he also explains how to get out of bad habits and create new ones that can lead you towards who you truly are.

These days, he can't *not* write. He made a choice to go for something he loved and he's not stopping.

All he really wants to do is tell stories, travel with his wife to oddball destinations by rickety transport, shoot baskets with his boys, try to perfect the burrito outside of California, and whisper the secrets of freedom and deep joy to whomever is within earshot and shares even the slightest inkling of curiosity.

There is more out there.

He currently lives in a little town outside of Utrecht in The Netherlands with his wife Saskia, famous two young boys of "The Adventures of Li & Lu" fame, and their at-least-as-famous dog Pepper.

This is Bradley's eighth book.

It is far, far, far from his last.

Find, ask, discuss, play at:
bradleycharbonneau.com

facebook.com/bradley.charbonneau.author

twitter.com/brathocha

instagram.com/brathocha

pinterest.com/likoma

bookbub.com/authors/bradley-charbonneau

CHARLIE HOLIDAY

Now Is Your Chance (1)

Second Chance (2)

Chance of a Lifetime (3)

FOR CREATIVES

Audio for Authors

Meditation for Creatives (2020)

SHORTS

Secret Bus to Paradise

Where I (Already) Am

Hungry?

A Trip to Hel

LI & LU

The Secret of Kite Hill (1)

The Secret of Markree Castle (2)

The Key to Markree Castle (3)

The Gift of Markree Castle (4)

Driehoek (5)

REALLY OLD ...

urban travel guide SAN FRANCISCO